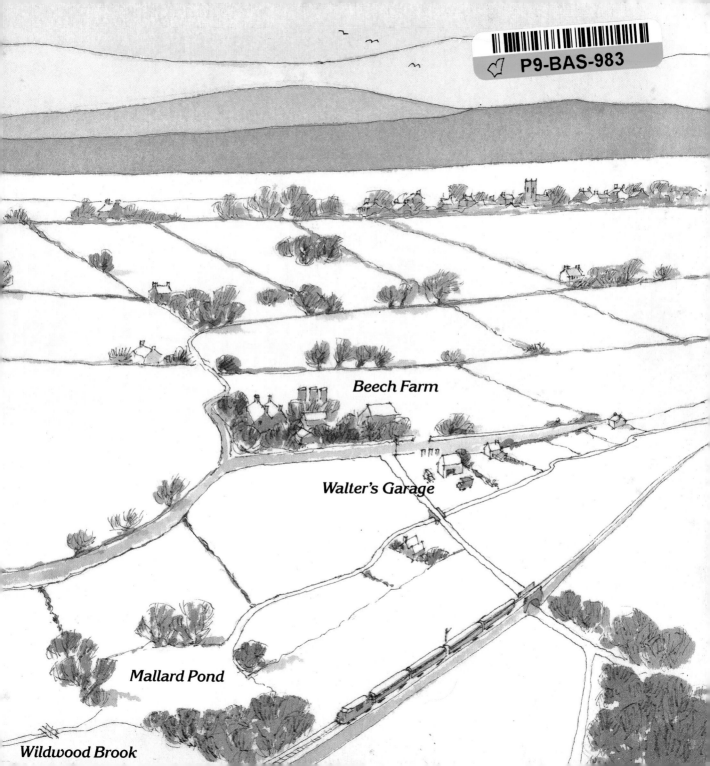

Beech Farm

Walter's Garage

Mallard Pond

Wildwood Brook

For Kerrie—C.R.

Text copyright © 1990 by Elizabeth Laird
Illustrations and characters copyright © 1990 by
Colin Reeder
First published in Great Britain
by William Collins Sons & Co. Ltd.

Tambourine Books,
a division of William Morrow & Company, Inc.,
1350 Avenue of the Americas, New York, New York 10019.
Printed in Portugal
First U.S. edition 1991
1   3   5   7   9   10   8   6   4   2

Library of Congress Cataloging in Publication Data
Laird, Elizabeth. The day the ducks went skating /
by Elizabeth Laird; illustrations by Colin Reeder.
p. cm— (A Little red tractor book)
Summary: Stan's reliable farm tractor Duncan comes in handy when
the ducks' pond freezes over and they cannot get to the water.
ISBN 0-688-10246-8 (trade)—ISBN 0-688-10247-6 (lib.)
[1. Tractors—Fiction.   2. Ducks—Fiction.   3. Farm life—
Fiction.]   I. Reeder, Colin, ill.   II. Title.   III. Series.
PZ7.L1579Das   1991   [E]—dc20   90-25899   CIP   AC

A Little Red Tractor Book

The Day the Ducks Went Skating

ELIZABETH LAIRD

pictures by COLIN REEDER

TAMBOURINE BOOKS · NEW YORK

The fields and fences of Gosling Farm were buried under a thick white blanket. The pale sunlight sparkled on icicles and drifting snow. It sparkled on some eager pink snouts too. The pigs were hungry. They could smell the lovely warm mash that Stan the farmer was tipping into their trough.

"Come on!" called Stan. "Come and get it!" And they did.

Back at the barn, the hens perked up their heads and clucked as Stan opened the big door. Duncan, the little red tractor, was cold. He'd never get started today. His battery felt as flat as could be!

"Bet you're cold this morning," said Stan. "Still, you'll have to get going, Duncan. The milking's done, and we must take the milk cans down the road. I just hope the truck gets through to pick them up. The snow's deep down by the bridge, I'll bet."

Stan climbed into the little tractor's cab, and turned the ignition key.
With a wheeze and a hiccup, Duncan's engine spluttered to life. He'd
done it! He'd started at the first try!

Stan hooked the trailer onto Duncan and drove him out of the
barn. The cans were full of fresh, creamy milk. Stan lifted them
onto the trailer, climbed back into Duncan's cab, and set off across
the snow.

It wasn't easy getting down the road. The ice was hard and slippery, and snow had drifted deep against the fences.

"Mind we don't skid by the old willow," said Stan. "I wouldn't be surprised if it's bad down there." Duncan took it slowly. Fumes puffed out of his exhaust pipe and made little white clouds in the frosty air.

Down by the farm gate, snow covered the milk stand. Stan scraped it off and set the cans on it. Then he looked up the road. There was no sign of the milk truck yet. He looked the other way. And then he noticed something.

"Oh, dear," he said, shaking his head. "There's a fox track, running up the road. After my hens, I'm sure. He must be hungry in this weather. I'd better get up to the barn again and see what's what."

Duncan started off up the road again. His wheels began to spin on the icy patches, but he kept on going. Stan tried to see where the fox had gone, but there were too many footprints crisscrossing the snow.

Was that the fox, lying in the bushes? No, it was only the shadow of a low-hanging branch. Were those his prints, crossing the field? No, it was only the trail of a rabbit.

Stan was worried. He pressed the accelerator, and the snow sprayed out from behind Duncan's rear wheels.

Stan jumped down from Duncan's cab and looked around the barn. The hens were quite happy, scratching and strutting in their usual way. There was no sign of the fox, thank goodness. He leaned over and switched off the engine.

Suddenly, everything was quiet. But then Stan heard something. There was a commotion at the bottom of Brookside Field. There was a quacking and a squawking down by the pond in the brook.

"That's him! He's after the ducks!" shouted Stan. He unhitched the trailer and jumped into Duncan's cab. Duncan started with a roar. There was no time to worry about skidding and slipping. Duncan was going full throttle.

Now Stan could see what the trouble was. The water was frozen over.
The ducks had nowhere to swim, and nowhere to dabble their beaks.
They could not get away from the hungry animal with the steely
teeth that circled round them on swift, silent feet, coming closer and
closer across the ice.

"Hey! Get out of there!" shouted Stan. "Go on, move it!"

The fox stopped in his tracks. He didn't like tractors. Tractors meant people, and people meant trouble. He turned and trotted away along the stream. He'd forget the ducks. But he would have to find a good dinner someplace else, before he grew weak with hunger.

The ducks were glad the fox was gone. They shook out their ruffled feathers and preened themselves.

Two old ducks waddled along the bank and poked about doubtfully with their beaks. They didn't approve of the snow.

The young ones loved it. One tried to take off on the frozen pond, slithered, skidded, and somersaulted, beak over tail. Another came in to land and shot along the ice, cackling with surprise.

Stan scratched his head. "I can't leave things like this," he said. "The fox'll be after the ducks again as soon as my back's turned."

He patted Duncan's steaming hood. "This is a job for you, Duncan," he said. "We'll have to see if you can break up the ice."

He climbed into Duncan's cab, and gently steered the little red tractor onto the ice. It cracked loudly, and splintered. The ducks took off with a clatter.

Duncan's engine roared as he rolled across the shallow, gravelly bed of the pool. Stan drove him round and round till the ice was all broken up. The ducks splash-landed with quacks of joy. They swam and dived and waggled their tails.

"I reckon they'll be all right now," said Stan. "We'll be back tomorrow if it freezes again."

He drove the little red tractor out onto the bank and turned away from the river. The sky had turned gray again, and great white snowflakes were falling.

Back at the farmyard, Stan jumped out of Duncan's cab. "There's so much work today," he said, "I don't know where to start."

Suddenly he stopped talking and looked up. There was a honking in the sky. A flock of geese flew low overhead, then dipped down to land on the clear water.

"Mallard Pond must be frozen over too," said Stan. "What a day this is for visitors!" He leaned over to wipe a splatter of slush off Duncan's windshield.

"We did a great job with the ice, didn't we, Duncan?" he said, and the little red tractor rumbled as if in agreement.

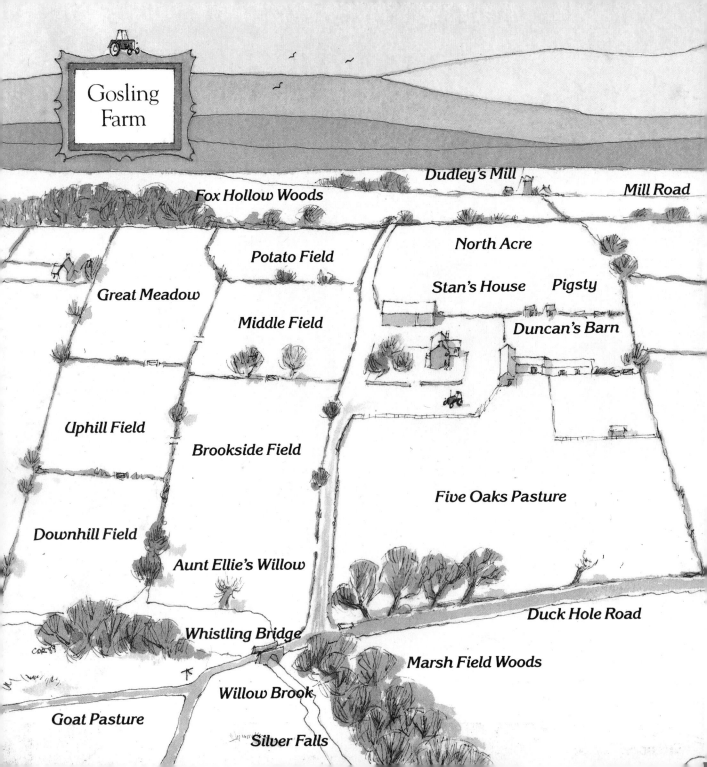

Gosling
Farm

Dudley's Mill

Mill Road

Fox Hollow Woods

North Acre

Potato Field

Stan's House   Pigsty

Great Meadow

Middle Field   Duncan's Barn

Uphill Field

Brookside Field

Five Oaks Pasture

Downhill Field

Aunt Ellie's Willow

Duck Hole Road

Whistling Bridge

Marsh Field Woods

Willow Brook

Goat Pasture

Silver Falls